T0145169

Jazzy and Rhumbi Become CHEFS

Special Thanks to
Louise Panelo, Kaye Parsons and Sid Wilson at Xlibris for all of their time
and care and special thanks to Henry MacAdam, husband and co-chef.

Illustrated by Schenker De Leon.

Other Books by this author:
A Place Called Happiness
Teach Me Something Real
Coincidence and Synchronicity
Flying To Breakfast, winner of the Pacific Book Review Five Star Award

Other Children's Books by this author:
Jazzy and Rhumbi To The Rescue
Jazzy And Rhumbi In Paris

Jazzy and Rhumbi would like to thank Chef Chris de Pagnier and Chef
Karen Child.

To order additional copies of this book, contact:
Xlibris
844-714-8691
www.Xlibris.com
Orders@Xlibris.com

ISBN: Softcover   978-1-6641-9058-0
          EBook   978-1-6641-9059-7

Print information available on the last page

Rev. date: 06/02/2022

Jazzy and Rhumbi Become CHEFS

DORI SEIDER

When we visited Paris, we, Jazzy Girl and Rhumbi Boy, two rescue cats who care very deeply about all animals, loved the moment that our chef came to the table next to us to give the dog food scraps and a bone. We thought that was very thoughtful and considerate.

We also loved the chef's hat and jacket, and how kind he was to us--stopping at our table to talk, asking us how we liked the food (it was scrumptious), and inviting us back.

The name of the restaurant was Chez Henri, which roughly translated, means Henry's Place. So now that we are home again, we decided to become chefs, to name our restaurant Chez Henri, and to serve wonderful comfort meals and desserts that we ourselves create.

Here is our first recipe, an international one which is easy to make.

Delicious Chicken Pita Sandwiches with Cucumber Dill Dressing:

Open up half of a pita bread and place chunks of cooked chicken inside

Put in a little bit of tomato, onion, and cucumber

For the Dressing:

Cut up a cucumber into tiny pieces and mix it with a cup of yogurt

Add some chopped dill

You can also add a teaspoon of lemon zest

Please Note: Get help in chopping and cutting. This dressing is called tzaziki.

We love being in the kitchen. Cooking and baking give us a big sense of accomplishment and they are fun to do. Also, every time you eat the healthy foods, you help your body to feel great.

Food can give you comfort and make you feel cozy on a cold, rainy day. For example, we love to make chicken soup on this kind of day. The aromas that waft through our little house are amazing. After we make our comforting, healthy chicken soup, we'll show you how to make another comfort food—banana bread.

Jazzy and Rhumbi's Healthy Chicken Soup

Place cut-up, cooked chicken in six cups of chicken broth

Add 3 cut up carrots, 3 cut up celery stalks, 3 cloves of, garlic and one big onion, cut in pieces

Add one-half teaspoon of the following spices:
turmeric, salt, pepper, and coriander (you can add more later, if desired)

Cook on medium heat for one hour, or simmer on low heat for two hours, or until done

Add a tablespoon of minced fresh parsley and/or fresh dill

Get help with chopping and cutting. Fine chopping is called mincing.

Most of us welcome a nice banana bread, warm out of the oven on cold days, or really on any day. This bread seems to make everyone happy no matter what. If you are not allergic to nuts, you can add one-half cup of chopped walnuts to the following recipe. You can also add one-half cup of dark chocolate chips.

Lillian's Banana Bread

2 cups of all-purpose flour
one teaspoon of baking powder
one teaspoon of baking soda
one-half cup of sugar
2 eggs, beaten
one-half cup of canola oil
3 small bananas mashed in one
tablespoon of vanilla
⅔ cup of plain yogurt
pinch of raw sugar and cinnamon,
mixed together to sprinkle on top

Add wet ingredients to dry ingredients. Bake at 350 degrees for 50-55 minutes in a loaf pan. It is done when a toothpick inserted comes out clean. You will notice that if you decide to add the pinch of raw sugar and cinnamon on top of the cake, it will come out nice and brown on top.

We hope you love those recipes as much as we do. You can always save them for any day you like. That's the beauty of the recipes in this book; you are free to use as few or as many as you like. You can also alter them to suit your taste.

For example, you could add cut up green pepper to your pita sandwiches, you can make the sandwiches all vegetables and no chicken, or you can add a different sauce that you make up yourself. For the soup, you can add different spices that you like and especially, you can put in some matzo balls. The easiest way to make these delicious, dumpling-like balls is to just buy a matzo ball mix at your supermarket, follow the directions, which include adding an egg, a little oil, and a little salt, put the mixture in the frig for 20 minutes or so and then form into balls. Get an adult human to carefully put them into the soup for you.

There are always variations you can do on any recipe, and the more you cook, you can think of more imaginative ways to make what you have already prepared several times before.

Speaking of variations, we, Jazzy Girl and Rhumbi boy, even though we are primarily named after music and dances, have secondary names of baked goods!

Not that this makes any logical sense, but our humans enjoy calling us Jazzy Girl Muffin and Rhumbi Boy Biscuit. I guess they love both music and food as much as we do! Be sure to look for the recipes called Jazzy Girl Muffins and Rhumbi Boy Biscuits later on in this book.

Our humans, The Quiet One and The Noisy Guy, like to cook in our home restaurant, Chez Henri just as much as we do. One day (before they got married and before they rescued us), they discovered a strange and wonderful coincidence—Noisy Guy had the crockpot cookbook but no crockpot. Quiet One had the crockpot, but no crockpot cookbook.

You may have heard of the expression: "There is a lid for every pot." But they actually had the exact book that went with the same crockpot! Sometimes the universe makes a point in a funny or ingenious way, just at the right time. Our humans have been cooking with this book and this pot for quite some time now and have taught us their skills. We would love to share with you our own recipe for crockpot beef stew. Hope you love it—it is easy to make, soothing and exceptionally tasty.

J and R Crockpot Beef Stew

Brown one pound of beef cubes in olive oil in a cast iron pan or another pan you like.

Cut up: 3 carrots, 3 sweet potatoes or red potatoes, one big onion, 3 cloves of garlic, one turnip if desired, one parsnip if desired and put all vegetables in the crockpot

Put the meat on top of the vegetables

Add one cup of water or broth

Set the crockpot to low, cover it and let it cook for 12 hours

If you want the stew sooner, set on high and let it cook for 4-5 hours

Get help from your humans, and always use mitts when you lift off the crockpot cover at the end.

Enjoy! Ymmmmmmmm!!!!!!!!!!!!!!

Yes, we love our crockpot, but there's something you don't know about us yet—we love kitchen gadgets, in general! Wait until we tell you about our happy little milk frother! A frother has a little part that whirs around in your cup.

Quiet One has always loved this little milk frother, but, one day, we thought it was irreparably broken. For one last time, the Noisy Guy tried to get it to work, but it definitely would not whir. Just as he was about to give up, he accidentally dropped it hard on the kitchen counter. Lo and Behold, it started to whir again, all on its own! Bzzzzzzz-- It just needed a shake-up! Who knew?

We ordered a new frother anyway, just to have back-up! Then we realized that we have a new opportunity for two guests at the same time to put the frother in their coffee or hot chocolate and make a great cappuccino or a whipped hot chocolate.

You never know with electronic equipment—sometimes, it just has a mind of its own. We are wondering what kitchen gadgets you may like?

Quiet One and Noisy Guy have a very old hand-held cake mixer and also an antique juice maker, where you cut the fruit in half and turn it around with your hand. They are very cherished.

But wait a minute! How about our blender, which makes healthy protein smoothies to have with all of these delicious creations?

Protein Smoothies

Place in a blender or Mixer of your choice

One cup of milk
1-2 scoops of protein power
One banana
One/half cup of frozen mixed berries
One-fourth cup of yogurt, frozen yogurt, or ice cream

Variation#1
Instead of a banana and berries, use an avocado and a handful of walnuts, to make an Avocado Walnut Smoothie

Variation#2
Make up your own combinations that you like

While we were writing our smoothie recipes for you, our friend Helen, who is 97 years old, called to say hello. We were so happy to hear from Helen! And also, we have always loved Helen's comfort tomato soup, so we decided to ask permission to put her recipe in this book. Not only did she say yes, but she helped us to explain the recipe to you. She is a wonderful friend as well as a superb cook.

Helen's Delicious Tomato Soup

Pour in 2 cans of beef broth

Add a large onion, 3 stalks of celery and 3 carrots and let them cook in the broth until softened

Take out the vegetables, but reserve the carrot to cut up and put back in the soup later

Add 2 cans of tomato soup and one can of crushed tomatoes and cook until the tomatoes mix thoroughly with the soup

Take out some of the soup and mix it with a little milk and a little half and half. (This mixing together with the soup and milk ingredients makes sure it doesn't curdle)Then add about one-half cup more milk and one-half cup more half and half, slowly and cook on low

When the soup is cooked and hot, before serving, add one cup of sour cream

Make elbow noodles separately, and when the soup is done, pour it over the noodles. Serve and enjoy!

Sit back and wait for all of the compliments to come in. Your guests will be totally comforted. As a matter of fact, they may feel transformed. They may say, mmmm, this is wonderful. You will think "Thank you, Helen!" And you may also be thinking that Helen is one of the nicest humans in the world of grateful cats and humans.

Now you may be thinking, "hey Jazzy and Rhumbi, how about my favorite comfort food, mac and cheese?" And we will tell you that we have anticipated this question and yes, we have tried to invent a healthier version of this dish. We know that you want creamy, velvety smooth, cheese-filled goodness, so we decided to continue that tradition and add some veggies as well. Remember that you, too, can make additions to any recipe and make it your own.

Jazzy and Rhumbi's Exquisite Macaroni and Cheese

Choose a different type of pasta and try it out. We have tried low-carb pasta, chickpea pasta, artichoke pasta and several others. If you are in a hurry, you can always use the macaroni pasta you have had before.

Have an adult human pour the box of pasta into boiling, salted water with a tablespoon of olive oil and let it cook.

When cool, taste a piece.

When it is "al dente" (has a bit of a bite) pour it into a casserole dish of your choice.

Add broccoli, carrots, celery, baby lima beans, mushrooms or any other veggies you like. Make sure they are cooked first. You can first sauté the veggies in olive oil, which will give them more flavor.

Put pieces of cheddar cheese on top, one-half cup of milk if desired and a cup of bread crumbs.

Bake at 350 degrees until the casserole is bubbly and the bread crumbs look toasty about 45 minutes.

Discuss what you would like to put into the mac and cheese with your cooking partner or your adult humans. Experiment many times until you get the perfect casserole for you.

When we were in Paris and went to a local bistro, they served a French country "potage" (soup) which did give us so much comfort on a snowy night, that it reminded us of mac and cheese. This potage is a French version of comfort food.

Imagine that you are back in Paris with us. It is cold and snowy and beautiful outside. You have just come from the Beauborg museum (the one with its big pipes on the outside) and you have just seen all of Paris in the snow from your view on top of the building. You then go to the little bistro where the following potage is being served. It is the perfect soup for this magical night.

French Country Potage, Jazzy and Rhumbi Style

Take 2 potatoes, 3 carrots and one onion (you can use a leek instead of the onion), and cook until soft. Have an adult human pour out the cooking water.

Purée the soft vegetables, by using a potato masher. When they are all mashed and look like a bowl of simple, mashed potatoes, add 2 pats of butter, enough milk or cream to look smoother (but still thick), salt and pepper to taste. Et Voilà! Élégante et délicieuse! (And there it is, elegant and delicious!)

Feel free to alter this soup to your taste. You can use an "immersion blender," if you have one. Ask an adult human to use this blender with you, and watch while the potatoes, carrots and leeks, or onion come together into a soothing soup!

Now, we know that you have waited quite a long time for some comforting desserts, too! No, of course we did not leave them out, so let's get to them right away! And what could be more comforting in the dessert realm, but things like pumpkin pie (with our own Jazzy and Rhumbi invented crust), blueberry and apple crumble, and all things chocolate? Let's begin with our pumpkin pie recipe.

Jazzy and Rhumbi's Just For You Pumpkin Pie

J and R Pie Crust:

Take 1 and a half cups of flour (If you are not allergic to nuts, you can use regular flour mixed with almond flour.) Of course, you can also use gluten-free flour.

Add two Tablespoons of Brown Coconut Sugar, or raw Sugar

Add one-fourth cup of canola oil or light olive oil with one egg in it, lightly beaten

Mix all together until it forms a ball and put it in the réfrigérateur (one of our favorite French words) for one-half hour.

Take out the dough ball, put it on a piece of waxed paper with a little flour on it and with a rolling pin that you also put a little flour on, roll it out and then place it in the pie pan.

Next, pour into the pie crust, a mixture of one 15 oz. can of pumpkin pureé, 2 eggs beaten, one quarter cup of brown coconut sugar, or raw sugar, a tablespoon of pumpkin pie spice, and two-thirds cup of evaporated milk.

Bake at 425 degrees for 15 minutes, then turn the temperature down to 350 degrees and bake for 40 more minutes.

Experiment with this recipe until you get your pumpkin pie the way you like it. Sometimes we look for alternate sugars because The Quiet One and The Noisy Guy are both lowering their sugar intake.

Pumpkin Pie Spice already has in it: cinnamon, nutmeg, clove and ginger. You can put them in separately also. We create a shortcut by using the Pumpkin Pie Spice, which already mixed them for us. We hope you love the pie as much as we do!

Now, crumbles, such as blueberry and apple, offer us a way to make comfort desserts easily and quickly. They are not as labor-intensive as pies, but taste just as good and are just as comforting.

Crumbles remind us of crockpot meals, where you just put everything into the crockpot and it cooks itself, in what feels like a total "onesy" experience. In crumbles, you put your fruit in the casserole, add a couple of quick things, then pour the topping on and bake. Let's try the blueberry one first.

J and R Perfect Comfort Blueberry Crumble

Put into a casserole dish: 2 cartons of fresh blueberries or 2-3 Packages of frozen blueberries.

Add zest of one lemon (ask an adult human to show you how to zest)

Add 2 tsp. vanilla

Add spices you love—cinnamon, nutmeg, a pinch of cloves or just add a Tablespoon of pumpkin pie spice

Sprinkle in one tablespoon of flour or ¼ cup of instant tapioca flakes for thickening

Pour a little water into the casserole

Topping:

One cup of flour, or gluten-free flour or almond flour
2 tsp. of sugar of your choice
One tablespoon of cinnamon
Optional: one cup of chopped walnuts

Mix in a half cup of butter or one fourth cup of oil, until a crumbly topping forms and sprinkle on fruit.

Bake at 350 degrees for about 50 minutes. It is done when it is all bubbly and the crumble is a little crisp

For Apple Crumble:

Use cut up apples instead of blueberries. The rest is the same—lemon zest, cinnamon. The crumble topping is the same.

We sometimes put a little apple juice on the bottom of the casserole, instead of water.

Bake time may be an hour, because the apples need to cook through.

You may choose to vary the spices, by just using cinnamon.

We, Jazzy and Rhumbi, served an apple crumble to one of our guests, named Shauna. She gasped when she saw how beautiful it came out. Needless to say, we were so pleased!

Rhumbi's Divine One Layer
Chocolate Cake

Mix together: 1 ½ cups of all-purpose flour and ½ cup of almond flour

one cup of unsweetened cocoa
2/3 cup of brown coconut sugar or raw sugar
1 teaspoon of baking powder
1 teaspoon of baking soda

Mix together:
2 eggs, beaten, ¼ cup of canola oil, ½ cup milk

Add the wet ingredients to the dry ingredients, mix with a hand mixer and bake in one round cake tin or one small square baking pan at 350degrees for 25-30 minutes

(Cake is done when a toothpick comes out clean)

If you want some *ganache* (an elegant French topping) it is very simple. Take a handful of dark chocolate chips, melt them in a microwave, and then add a little half and half until it looks like cake frosting. After the cake is cool, spread the *ganache* over the top.

We bet that you would love our tartelettes. In english, they are just called tarts, but in french, a tart is a whole pie, and a tartelette is a little pie, or tart. When we were in Paris, we would stop at a pâtisserie (pastry shop) either on our way somewhere or on our way back. These tarts made with real fruit, were always so colorful and so delicious!

Les Tartelettes

You will need little tart pans or muffin tins.

The simplest way to make tartelettes is to crumble up your favorite cookies (they can even be chocolate cookies), add a Tablespoon of butter and bake at 350 degrees for 3-5 minutes

When they cool, add some tapioca or vanilla pudding, then add some cut-up fruit.

You can design the pieces of fruit any way you want—this is where your creativity comes in.

They are great to look at and great tasting!

Maybe you don't want a sweet pie, but you want a little pie with real food in it. The inside food can be veggies or meat and veggies. These are so delicious. They are sometimes called "pasties," "pockets," "empanadas" or other names. Especially good on a cold day or as comfort food on any day, these little pies are child-size. Make sure they are not too hot if you are going to hold them in your hands with a napkin. Also ask an adult human for help when you make these. Try it different ways until you get exactly what you want. Then write it down and keep it in a handy place so that you can find it easily next time.

Food Pies

Make an easy dough for the pie crust, using one cup of flour, ¼ cup of oil, a pinch of salt, if desired, and an egg, which will hold it all together. (The flour can be gluten-free)

Put into the little pie crust dough some cooked chicken and vegetables and some thick soup. (You can use turkey or beef) Put fork holes or little slits into the dough and bake at 350 degrees for 45 minutes or until the crust is browned

Let it cool down a little and then Enjoy!

Most people love fried potatoes, and so do we, Jazzy and Rhumbi. We decided to try a healthier version, though, baked sweet potato fries. We are always on the look-out for ways to make things that are utterly scrumptious, but made in a healthier way, and made with less salt and sugar than many other recipes. This way we can eat deliciously and still feel nourished with vitamins and minerals. Sweet potatoes have lots of vitamin A and other healthy things.

Now, do you remember when we, Jazzy and Rhumbi went to the Viennese café in Paris and met our relatives for coffee and apple strudel? Even if you don't remember this, we want to share our recipe for real apple strudel with you.

It is so much fun, because you get to actually stretch the dough with your fingers! And you can go around the table stretching the dough, if possible. Don't worry if it stretches a little too much in places and you get a hole—you can always fill the hole with dough later.

Before you even make the dough, you can decide on what fillings you want-sliced apples, cinnamon, raisins, lemon rind, are a few suggestions.

Making strudel is an art that goes way back, and our grandmothers may know it best, but don't get intimidated—it really is easier than it sounds. Also, if you are in a hurry, you can use phyllo dough, fill it and bake—voilà!

Jazzy and Rhumbi's Real Apple Strudel

For the crust:
1 and ¼ cup flour
butter
egg
lukewarm water or milk

Mix your dough and then knead it. Roll it out with a rolling pin, then gently stretch each side with your fingers. Keep stretching until it gets thinner and thinner. When it is large, thin and flat, put the filling all over it and then roll the strudel up around the filling.

Take the whole "tube" of strudel, make it into a crescent shape, if you want, and place it on a nonstick cookie sheet. Bake at 350 degrees for one hour.

If you are in a hurry, you can use phyllo dough, fill it, roll it over the filling and bake. Unbelievably delicious!

We hope that you have enjoyed many of the recipes in this book. We loved sharing them with you! Cooking and baking are often much easier than they sound.

Everyone can cook and bake well, young and old. You will probably find that everyone enjoys your cooking and baking so much that they will often ask for second helpings. They will also ask you to cook and bake more and they will volunteer to be "taste-testers."

The soups, crumbles, cakes and pastries that you make can always be shared with others, or just given away to them. Our neighbors have often brought over whole cakes or pies to surprise us! Making nourishing food and desserts gives you a chance to be a giver. We, Jazzy Girl and Rhumbi Boy love to give all the time.

Cooking and baking make us feel super-competent also, giving us a deep feeling of accomplishment and satisfaction. Also, think of the aromas that will waft all through your house!

Jazzy Girl Muffins

2 cups flour

¼ to ½ cup raw sugar or coconut sugar

1 teaspoon baking powder

2 eggs

⅓ cup oil

one cup chocolate chips of your choice, (semisweet or bittersweet)

Preheat oven to 350 degrees

Mix your dry ingredients.

In a smaller bowl, beat egg in oil and add milk.

Pour your wet ingredients into your dry ingredients and stir, without overmixing.

Add chocolate chips.

Put batter into a muffin tin with paper muffin cups, or into a greased muffin tin and bake for 20-25 minutes or so, until a toothpick comes out clean.

Cool for 5-10 minutes.

Yield: 12 muffins.

Rhumbi Boy Biscuits

2 cups flour

1 Tablespoon baking powder

¼ tsp. salt (optional)

5 Tablespoons of chilled butter, cut into pieces

¾ cup milk or buttermilk(if you use buttermilk, add ½ teaspoon of baking soda to the recipe, and try 6 tablespoons of butter instead of 5)

Like the other recipes, experiment until you like your unique result.

Preheat oven to 425 degrees

Add butter to flour and mix until it makes big crumbs, add milk until just combined. The dough will be sticky.

Put dough on floured surface and knead for 30 seconds (push dough with your palms)

Roll out the dough and then cut circles with a biscuit cutter or paper cup.

Put biscuits on an ungreased baking sheet and bake for 12-20 minutes, until golden brown.

Jazzy and Rhumbi are serving their guests in their country dining room. The round table is olive green.

Their guests are: 3 cats of different colors and breeds, 1 dog, and 2 humans, The Quiet One and The Noisy Guy. They are all chatting and smiling and having a wonderful time. On the table is: an apple strudel, some muffins and a one layer chocolate cake with some chocolate ganache dripping from the top.

We have loved sharing our baking and cooking ideas with you, and we hope you have many happy times doing both. We also hope that you will read this book over and over with joy, laughter, good health and much satisfaction.

Jazzy and Rhumbi To The Rescue — Book Review

This heartwarming and adventurous tale is told from the perspective of two resourceful kitties named Jazzy Girl Muffin and Rhumbi Boy. These compassionate cats secretly influence their humans to love and rescue more animals.

A colorful compilation of anecdotes dedicated to the precious animal lives surrounding us, Seider's work introduces the reader to two lovable cats whose adventures are certain to charm and delight. With an excellent message to share with children of all ages, the adorable narrative, complete with PAW 5s and humorous asides from the perspective of two well-loved kitties, ensures that the message is playful and never preachy. Children and adults will love Jazzy and Rhumbi and their heartfelt message and will undoubtedly eagerly await their adventures to come.

- US Review of Books

Printed in the United States
by Baker & Taylor Publisher Services